WHATSOEVER YOU DO

From The Earth Series
Book 1

D.W. PATTERSON

Twenty-First Printing – July 2026

Future Chron Publishing

Hard Science Fiction – Old School.

To Sarah

WHATSOEVER YOU DO

CHAPTER 1

Miri first noticed the baby's symptoms that morning, a wheezing sound when he exhaled. By afternoon Miri was worried enough to call the pediatrician.

A nurse set up an appointment for the next day and instructed Miri to keep Jack Jr. hydrated and his nasal passages clear, with a bulb syringe if necessary. She told Miri to take the baby to the emergency room if symptoms worsened before the appointment.

By the time Jack got home from the university that evening Jack Jr. seemed a little better. But Jack's usual cheerful smile evaporated as Miri told him about the baby's illness.

"What did the doctor say?" asked Jack, stroking his son's cheek.

"I set up an appointment for tomorrow. The nurse said to give him plenty of fluids and keep his nasal passages clear."

She turned away and coughed as Jack tried to kiss her.

"You don't sound too good yourself. I hope you're taking something."

"Same thing as the baby," she said.

They were preparing to turn in for the night when Miri's smartphone alerted. She took a look at the phone and started for the nursery.

Jack heard her yell for him to come quickly. When he walked into the nursery he saw Miri with Jack Jr. in her arms.

She turned and said, "We have to get him to the emergency room, his breathing is rapid and shallow and he's not waking up!"

Jack looked at his son and shuddered. He was sure the baby's lips had a bluish tinge.

"Okay honey. Wrap him up and bring him into our bedroom, I'm getting dressed."

Jack already had his pants and shirt on and was pulling on his socks when Miri walked into the room.

"Give him to me honey while you change.”

Miri handed over the baby and rushed into her closet.

Jack looked at his son and almost cried out, the baby's fingernails were turning blue. Jack knew his boy wasn't getting enough oxygen - they would have to hurry. He fought to maintain his composure. If he panicked Miri might also, but he couldn't wait another minute.

"Miri! Meet me at the car."

Jack placed his sleeping son on the passenger's seat and put the car in manual mode. He backed it out of the garage, his right hand never leaving his son's chest. The time he spent listening to the baby's labored breathing seemed like an eternity to Jack even though Miri arrived moments later.

“Please hurry,” she said as she took the baby in her arms.

“We'll be there soon,” said Jack placing his hand on her shoulder.

Miri was about to acknowledge but turned her head away to cough.

The emergency room was crowded. The admitting nurse was about to hand Jack and Miri paperwork to fill out when she saw the baby's face. She immediately stopped what she was doing and yelled to another nurse to take the Jackson's into an examination room while she called for a doctor.

Doctor Stilhs entered the examination room, took a quick look at Jack Jr. and said, “Mr. and Mrs. Jackson would you please step into the waiting room? I'll be there as soon as I've finished my examination, thank you.”

Jack and Miri looked at each other and turned to leave. Miri looked back at the doctor.

“As soon as possible doctor, please,” she said.

The doctor nodded.

It was almost an hour before the doctor came into the waiting room.

“I was beginning to worry doctor, what have you found?” asked Jack.

“Mr. and Mrs. Jackson your son has a bronchial infection. I've ordered tests but it will be an hour or more before we have the results. Meanwhile I've also ordered that he be given fluids and oxygen to prevent dehydration and help him breathe. We'll know more when we get the tests back.”

“He's going to be okay isn't he doctor?” asked Miri, coughing to clear her throat.

“Mrs. Jackson I'm afraid your son is very sick, but he seems strong and I think there is every reason to believe that he will recover. But it sounds like you may be coming down with something yourself, you should try to get some rest.”

“Thank you doctor,” said Jack.

After the doctor left Jack and Miri sat down.

“We should do as the doctor says honey. You need rest before you get any worse, and I think you could rest better at home.”

“Jack, I cannot leave this hospital as long as my son is in here. I'm staying.”

“Okay honey, I understand. Let's try to make ourselves as comfortable as possible.”

He gently guided her head to his shoulder.

The morning light was flooding through the hospital window when Jack awoke. Miri was asleep beside him, her breathing labored. Jack got up carefully and went to ask the nurse for some coffee. By the time he returned with two cups Miri had awakened.

“Good morning honey, how are you feeling?”

Just then an orderly rushed up.

“Mr. and Mrs. Jackson?” he asked.

“Yes,” said Jack.

“The doctor wants to see you, follow me please.”

Jack and Miri followed the man to a different exam room from before, there they found the doctor waiting. He looked like he hadn't slept.

“Mr. and Mrs. Jackson, I'm so sorry. Your son died just a few minutes ago.”

Miri fainted.

CHAPTER 2

As a young engineering student, Jack had been part of a research group that was developing an integrated circuit with the goal of running complex neural networks on a mobile platform. The platform would host a software-based Artificial Narrow Intelligence (ANI), commonly called an Annie.

Jack's specialty on the team was packing the necessary functions into a three-dimensional substrate while maintaining performance requirements. He developed what he called the Matryoshka (Russian nesting dolls) approach to help meet the requirements. Jack became famous on the team for writing the software that met packing and performance compliance.

He was still an undergraduate working with the Annie group when his son died. His wife succumbed a short time later. Jack thought Miri had lost her will to live after their son died. Both Miri and Jack Jr. had been early victims in a viral pandemic that took the lives of millions.

Jack vowed to not let it happen again.

He immediately changed majors to pursue biological research in infectious diseases. His single-minded focus enabled him to pack seven years into five, and he soon found himself the youngest researcher at a very prestigious university. He would find a cure for those like his son and wife who caught the virus early before the need for a vaccine was even apparent. Jack loved his research, but even so, it was becoming a strain because of the pressure for results put upon him by his adviser.

It was late at night, and Jack was working alone in the lab as usual. He was working at the synthetic biology station. Jack had chosen to use synthetic biology because of its engineering approach, which could be applied to biological systems. Synthetic biology held the promise of fast and easy design of biological systems instead of the usual trial and error method most biologists were familiar with. Well defined biological building blocks were used to assemble biological systems much as one could use electronic components to design a useful electronic circuit.

Jack was using synthetic biology to develop a synthetic gene circuit that could function outside a cell and could quickly identify viral agents. It would be embedded in paper for testing. He hoped by creating this paper-based detector it would serve as a proof of concept for his approach.

Suddenly, as he bent over the station he felt a hot flash of pain in his skull, like an explosion. The pain increased and lasted more than a minute before it subsided. By that time Jack found himself sitting on the floor.

When he recovered enough to stand, he secured his experiment and closed up the lab. As he walked to the curb, he took his Annie out of his pocket and unfolded it.

"Yes Jack," said the Annie.

Jack explained his symptoms and asked the Annie what might have happened to him. The Annie took his vitals from his wrist band and ran its medical expert. It called for an Ark-car to take him to the hospital.

The self-navigating car arrived and as it drove him to the hospital he listened to the Annie conjecture about his health. At the hospital, he ended up being admitted for observation.

The next morning a doctor came into Jack's hospital room.

"Mr. Jackson?"

"Yes."

"I have to tell you Mr. Jackson that was a reckless thing to do, driving by yourself to the hospital instead of calling for an ambulance. What if you had another attack with no medical personnel around?"

"Well sir, I guess I wasn't exactly thinking straight after such an episode, have you ever had such an attack?"

"I have not," said the doctor, softening somewhat. "I guess I would be a bit confused myself under similar circumstances. By the way, I'm Doctor Greyson, I'll be your attending physician."

"So, what do you think happened to me? I feel fine now."

"I believe you had a transient ischemic attack. Sometimes called TIA or a mini-stroke."

"My Annie suggested that was a possibility, but I thought that a stroke was something that usually happened to older people?"

"That is generally the case. But it can also happen to anybody at any time in their life. It could be caused by an inherited risk, it could be lifestyle choices, or it could be an imbalance of an amino acid, specifically homocysteine levels in your blood; or it could be all of the above. That is what we are going to find out. I've ordered the necessary tests and questionnaires for you to fill out."

Dr. Greyson turned to leave but looked back to say, "Please be honest when filling out the forms, the diagnosis depends on it."

Jack had answered the questionnaires as accurately as he could through the data diagnostics Annie. The results would be run through another ANI program and combined with his medical history to make a preliminary diagnosis for the doctor. Jack had also had an MRI and a complete blood workup. And now he was told that another test had been ordered and an intelligent gurney would be here any moment to take him to the exam room. The I-gurney finally showed up an hour later. He queried the robot about what test was scheduled next.

"Don't you know?" asked the I-gurney.

"No. No one has told me anything except that I had another test scheduled."

"Oh dear, I thought you knew. You are scheduled for an angiogram of the carotid artery in your neck. Let me see here," said the I-gurney accessing the hospital's database.

"Mr. Jackson, it says here that your carotid could have caused your attack. Therefore, the test. This may take some time; you should try to visit the restroom now."

Three hours later Jack was back in his room and starving. It was late in the day and because of the tests, he hadn't been allowed to eat any breakfast. He begged the floor nurse to bring him some food, the nurse agreed. The robotic food butler showed up with a small bowl of apple sauce and a slice of bread. Jack was just about to beg the food butler for more when Doctor Greyson came in.

"Well Mr. Jackson, I've reviewed the tests and questionnaires and data history from your wrist band, and I believe you did have a transient ischemic attack as I said this morning. The levels of homocysteine in your blood are high. You also have other lifestyle risks that we need to address."

"What do you mean, lifestyle risks?"

"You seem to have an all work and no play profession Mr. Jackson. It's widely believed that contributing factors to TIA are a sedentary lifestyle and high stress. All work and no play, you know. Also, I suspect your diet is not as varied as it should be in fruits and vegetables. Would I be correct in that assumption?"

"I guess so. It's true that I have put my work above everything else in my life for the last five years. But I have my reasons."

"I'm sure you do Mr. Jackson but this attack should be taken as a warning. You are at high risk for a stroke in the next six months; a stroke that would probably end whatever you are trying to accomplish at work. So, we need to start now to reduce that risk."

"What do you mean?"

"We will use gene therapy to repair any cell damage you may have suffered but I would still suggest that you plan a sabbatical from your work to reduce your stress level."

Jack was quiet.

Finally he said, "That's quite a choice you are offering me doctor. My work means everything to me. But as you say I won't finish it if I have a stroke."

He sighed, “I'll need some time to think. Would a month be a good rest interval?”

“I would suggest six months Mr. Jackson. At the end of that time if you've followed all my recommendations and the homocysteine level is in an acceptable range, then a reasonable work schedule could be resumed. A balanced work-life would be possible.”

“I see. Thank you doctor.”

“Okay Mr. Jackson, I'm going to recommend your release. I have ordered some prescriptions for you, the nurse will explain your treatment regimen. You should be ready to go home in about an hour.”

After the doctor closed the door Jack sighed.

Oh Miri, what now?

CHAPTER 3

Eleven hours on an airplane were more than enough, but Wesley Williams still had nearly three hours before he landed at Addis Ababa International Airport in Ethiopia. He had tried to sleep but he could only achieve an hour or two at a time. In between his naps, he studied the case book prepared for him.

Wesley was a researcher at the National Center for Emerging Infectious Diseases at the Centers for Disease Control and Prevention (CDC) in Atlanta, USA. He had been sent to Juba, South Sudan at the request of a doctor with the Doctors International Outreach (DIO) organization to investigate what seemed to be a new viral outbreak.

Wesley hadn't any idea where the state of South Sudan was until he was well on his way to Africa. The layover in Addis Ababa would allow Wesley to do some advance scouting. But for now, he went back to sleep.

Wesley awoke as the plane touched down. He was soon in the main concourse of Addis Ababa International. Except for the occasional sign, a traveler might never know where he was in the world. The airport was as modern as any Wesley had ever seen. He queried his Annie as to the location of his hotel in Juba, where the Ministry of Health was located and where the DIO clinic was located. The clinic was his main objective while staying in the capital city. The Annie was slow to respond. Obviously, the cloud connection was limited. By the time it was finishing with his request Wesley was dozing off again.

He awoke in time to hear the call for his flight. The plane was an older prop model, and he had to walk across the tarmac and climb the boarding steps. By the time the plane was in the air, he had dozed off again to the sound of the propeller engines.

The bumpy landing which woke him was an immediate indication that things would be different in Juba. Departing the plane Wesley noticed that he was surrounded by United Nations,

World Food Program, and Russian cargo jets parked in a close jumble because of the limited size of the apron. It was obvious that foreign aid and foreign influence was still important to South Sudan even after years of independence.

If Wesley thought the parking apron small, the room he found himself in for visa check, baggage collection, customs and passport control was about the size of a large living room in the United States. It was crowded, hot and chaotic. Somewhere to the side, he saw his name on a sign. He motioned to the young man to meet him in the middle of the crush of people.

The young man had been sent by DIO and was to take Wesley to his motel, but first, they had to get him through customs. He led Wesley to the visa window where there didn't seem to be a queue. Passport, entry permit and a crisp American hundred dollar note, and they were off to retrieve the luggage. After some shoving, loud arguing in English, Dinka and Nuer with a smattering of Arabic pidgin, the luggage was retrieved.

Wesley by now was impressed with the young man's skills and followed him to the customs area. There both bags were opened, actually spilled onto a table, searched and then chalked, apparently meeting with the custom officer's approval, Wesley was allowed to repack his bags after another hundred-dollar bill exchanged hands.

Now it was a fight to get to the immigration official who checked Wesley's passport and the chalked luggage again and accepted a hundred dollar "tip," before allowing him to move into the arrivals area. Once Wesley found his baggage tag from Addis Ababa, he was allowed to leave the one-room terminal.

Outside the terminal, the young man found his motorbike where he had left it chained. He looked relieved to find the bike in order. As they had a moment the young man introduced himself.

"I am Kamal Cham Dr. Williams, I will be your guide during your stay here in Juba," he said in almost perfect English.

"I am very glad to meet you Kamal," said Wesley. "I really

am impressed with your expertise in guiding me through that ordeal."

"I have done it many times."

"I have to ask though, to whom do I owe the three hundred dollars?"

"Do not worry Dr. Williams. It is the cost of doing business here. Dr. Petiot will charge it against expenses. Shall we go now?"

"Yes," said Wesley.

They put Wesley's bags in the small cart attached to the back of the motorbike. Wesley climbed on to the rear of the extra-long seat. The seat was long enough for several people as Wesley confirmed by noticing other boda-bodas with three to four people climbing onto them. The ride to the Panorama Hotel was just over a mile distant.

Kamal left Wesley at the front desk after making arrangements to pick him up early in the morning for the trip to the Ministry of Health where Wesley would present himself as a courtesy to the authorities. Wesley had a quick bite to eat in the hotel's restaurant and retired to his room, which unlike the ordeal of the flight and Juba airport, wasn't that bad.

Wesley took out his Annie and unfolded it. He asked for the weather for tomorrow in Juba. The Annie cautioned that connections to the cloud were very tenuous, it might take a while for it to fulfill his request. Wesley told his Annie that it could go offline and he would check in the morning for the answer. He quickly washed and went to bed.

The following morning, after leaving the Ministry of Health, Kamal and Wesley were on their way to the DIO clinic. So far Juba, except for its awful connection to the cloud, had not been too far out of the ordinary for Wesley. The streets were paved, trees though not plentiful lined some blocks, but this was about to change.

Kamal turned onto a side street west of the Ministry and

headed south. The character of the buildings began to change. They looked older and worse kept than what Wesley had previously seen. Then as Kamal turned west again the pavement ended and the street became dusty red dirt. The bike kicked at the ruts and Wesley held on to the seat. They finally arrived at the clinic which was not much different than the surrounding buildings except for the sign and the fresh coat of white-wash which was quickly becoming red-tinged from the ground up.

Dr. Petiot, a small man in a white smock, came out to greet them.

"Welcome Dr. Williams," he said with a slight French accent. "And thank you Kamal, for bringing our guest safely. How are you Dr. Williams? Is there anything I can get for you, such as food?"

"No thank you Dr. Petiot," said Wesley. "And please call me Wesley."

"And you shall call me Jacques."

"Very good. As you know I have only a day to investigate your request and obtain any samples I might need. Are we prepared to tour the facilities?"

"Of course, follow me please."

The clinic was well maintained and seemed to be properly supplied, though it would have been considered primitive in Europe or the States. Dr. Petiot took Wesley immediately to the corridor that housed the suspect patients.

"At this time, we have about a dozen patients with the same symptoms," said Dr. Petiot. "As I stated in my request to the CDC the symptoms start with a headache and burning eyes. This gives way to fever and disturbed sleep. In the worse cases, they begin to drift in and out of consciousness, complaining of muscle aches and their head throbbing. If we are unable to stop the disease's progression their face will start to change color to a darkish purple-brown. Soon they begin coughing up blood and eventually gasp for air as they drown, their lungs overwhelmed with bloody fluid. We have lost eleven out of the twenty-six patients we've treated."

"Certainly, sounds like a virus," said Wesley. "In the terminal cases, how long does it take to run its course?"

"Anywhere from twenty-four to thirty-six hours."

"Really! That fast?"

"Yes, and it is usually the young healthy patients that go quickly. That should sound familiar."

"Yes, it does. Just like the last viral outbreak a few years ago. Except the time from contracting the illness to death has been compressed."

"Yes, and this viral outbreak doesn't seem as contagious, thank goodness," said Dr. Petiot.

Wesley spent the rest of the day visiting with patients and the other doctors and nurses at the clinic. He used his Annie and sensor attachments to make a preliminary investigation of blood, tissue, and fluids from the infected patients. The difficulty of getting a good cloud connection prevented the Annie from making a quick diagnosis but a virus was definitely the main suspect. The clinic's technicians, under Wesley's supervision, prepared further samples for him to take back to the CDC for testing.

CHAPTER 4

The day after Jack was released from the hospital, he called his thesis adviser to arrange a few days off, and to schedule a meeting with him for the following week to further discuss his situation. He hadn't been off the call very long when his Annie alerted him to an incoming call from Phylicia Hastings. Phylicia was a fellow grad student in his lab.

"Hi Jack, its Phylicia, I just heard that you won't be coming to work for a while. Is something wrong?"

A first-year doctoral candidate, Phylicia Hastings' specialty was DNA sequencing and gene expression. She was short, quick-witted and had a knack for knowing who to call to solve a problem.

“Doing okay at the moment,” said Jack. “But a couple of days ago I was working late in the lab and suddenly got a bad headache, the next thing I know I'm on the floor. It turned out to be a mini-stroke.”

"Oh no! That must have been a terrible ordeal, so unexpected at your age. Is there anything I can do for you?"

"No, nothing that I can think of. I'm just supposed to rest. I'll be in next week to speak with Professor Camble about what I need to do to recover.”

"Well please be sure to look me up while you're here. I'll probably be in my office, if not, look in the lab. Will you promise to call if you need anything in the meantime?"

"Alright I'll stop by, and thanks.”

Jack had always found Phylicia helpful and upbeat, but he had never considered her a close friend, so it was a little surprising but somehow comforting to hear from her. He had no one else.

Jack spent the next several days thinking about how he could follow the doctor’s orders while still pursuing his research. He soon settled into his new routine with his Annie providing scheduling and diet support. He reviewed his finances and found that if he was careful, he should have enough savings to last for several months. He hadn't made much as a researcher, but he hadn't spent much either.

In reviewing his past, Jack came to realize that he had gotten caught up in the business of doing science. He had become so engrossed in grant proposals, publishing, conference presentations and team building, that the core of science, theory and experimentation, was something he did almost as an aside. All that activity had the appearance of progress but in fact, it was no more than a cycle of busyness. He had gotten caught up in that cycle and he now realized that many of his fellow researchers were also.

If only he had applied some of the engineering discipline he had learned as an undergraduate. He might have more to show for his efforts.

Miri had been right about him always rushing through everything without looking back. 'A roller coaster ride', she called his approach to life, always looking for the next thrill. He had dismissed her concerns as unfounded worry. Hadn't she understood that all the hard work was just a means to an end? To hurry the coming of the day when he could slow down and spend more time with her and little Jack. Now his health had imposed upon him the necessity of slowing down, reviewing his days, and planning his tomorrows.

Jack's eyes watered.

Miri, without you and little Jack what do I have to plan for?

CHAPTER 5

After his day at the clinic, Wesley prepared to depart.

"Thank you and your staff Jacques. You've been most accommodating. I have to say I'm impressed with the work you are doing here for the Sudanese people."

"You are welcome, Wesley. You will keep me informed of the findings of the CDC?"

"Absolutely, and thanks again."

His sample bag already secured to the motorbike by Kamal, Wesley climbed aboard and they were off to the hotel.

Juba was located close to tropical forests along the White Nile. But this section of Juba, with its dirt roads and few trees and small scrub bushes, reminded Wesley very much of the western part of America, only with a lot more red dirt which was everywhere, even in the air. As he looked at the bare concrete buildings they passed, he noticed for the first time a military presence. Soldiers standing guard at each intersection. Soldiers gathered at the entrance to commercial buildings. He didn't remember seeing them on the way out that morning.

Kamal dropped Wesley off at the Panorama and confirmed that he would pick him up the next morning for the trip to the airport.

As a backup to his Annie, Wesley asked the desk clerk for a wake-up call at six the following morning and went to his room. He placed the samples in the small fridge, and once secured, he went to the dining room for dinner before emailing the CDC and turning in for the night.

Wesley awoke to what sounded like thunder. He asked his Annie for the time. It was a few minutes after five. He snapped awake when he heard the unmistakable sharp crack of gunfire. A more distant thunder made him sit up; he jumped at the knock on the door.

Wesley went to the door and demanded, "Who's there?"

"It's me Kamal."

Kamal entered the room. "Hurry Dr. Williams. We must get you out of here and to the airport before the roads are blocked."

"Okay Kamal, while I get dressed tell me what's happening?"

"The Dinka's are attacking the Nuers. The government forces are trying to stay neutral."

"Why? Why doesn't the government maintain order?"

"The government is caught in the middle. It is a coalition with no side having a clear majority. So, they cannot generate a consensus and they do nothing. It's tribal, I have seen it many times."

Wesley had his clothes on and, having packed before bed last night, was almost ready. All he had to do was get the samples from the room fridge. When finished he turned to Kamal and said, "I'm ready."

They climbed aboard the motorbike for the short trip up Airport Road. But Kamal immediately turned onto a side street. He yelled back at Wesley, "The main roads are probably already blocked; we will take a less direct route."

"You know best," yelled Wesley over the roar of the motorbike.

Only a couple of blocks had passed, when they almost crashed into a military convoy. the convoy roaring through the crossroads. The last jeep in the convoy slid to a stop. Two soldiers jumped out with their guns trained on Kamal and Wesley.

"Halt!" they yelled in Dinka. "Who are you, where are you going?"

Kamal answered in Dinka, "I am Kamal Cham and this is Dr. Wesley Williams from America. I am taking the doctor to the airport to catch his plane."

The soldiers approached the pair. "Why then are you going

this way? It is quicker and shorter by Airport Road."

"We were worried that the road might be blocked," said Kamal.

"Maybe," said one of the soldiers. "Get off the bike we need to search."

One of the soldiers was inspecting Wesley's passport and identification. The other had taken Wesley's bags back to the jeep to search. Just as he reached the jeep a shot rang out. The soldier dropped. The bags hit the ground. Then the concussion of an explosion launched the jeep into the air and made Wesley hit the ground and scramble for his papers, which the remaining soldier had thrown down when he started running.

Kamal had mounted and started the motorbike, when he yelled at Wesley to get on. Wesley struggled to his feet and climbed behind Kamal.

"My bags, Kamal my bags!" he yelled.

"Sorry doctor," yelled Kamal as he gunned the motorbike. "I'm afraid they have been destroyed, we must go."

Kamal slid the bike around the corner of the street as the remains of the jeep were blocking the intersection. He righted the cycle and opened the throttle. Wesley was too shocked at what had just happened to be afraid of the speeding, careening motorbike.

Wesley noticed all the lights on the streets and the buildings were out. In the distance, he could see the orange-red glow of fire. He still heard a loud boom occasionally, but thankfully in the distance. Kamal pitched the bike over as he made another turn without slowing. Wesley had no idea where he was or which way was the airport.

Just then they turned onto Airport Road and Wesley saw the airport entrance. Kamal had succeeded.

Kamal had to stop at the makeshift checkpoint that had been set up. The guard challenged him. Kamal, speaking in Nuer answered back. The guard looked at Wesley and asked in English for his papers. Finally, they were allowed to pass.

Wesley was still stunned when Kamal pulled up to the entrance and stopped.

"Sorry, Dr. Williams, about your bags. I'm afraid there was nothing I could do."

"You did everything you could Kamal," said Wesley somewhat in shock. Artillery boomed nearby.

"I want to thank you for getting me here safe, it's unfortunate about the bags but it's not your fault."

"Goodbye Doctor," said Kamal as he started his motorbike and roared away.

Wesley stared in disbelief at the back of the disappearing Kamal, riding away almost as if nothing had happened.

He walked up to the guard at the entrance to the airport lobby. He pulled his papers and identification from his coat pocket. The guard allowed him to pass.

CHAPTER 6

The meeting with Professor Camble had gone well, Jack thought. He had explained that he wouldn't be able to come back for at least six months, doctor's orders. Professor Camble had been understanding, and told Jack he had his full support, and that Jack's health was the most important thing. Jack left the meeting feeling confident that someday he would be able to return to his research at the university.

Jack went looking for Phylicia, finding her in her office. They decided to get a cup of coffee in the cafeteria before her next appointment.

"How did the meeting with Professor Camble go?" asked Phylicia after they were seated.

"He was actually very understanding. I was afraid that he might be upset when I told him I would have to take six months off."

"Six months!" exclaimed Phylicia before she could catch herself. "I'm sorry Jack, I didn't mean to, I mean it is such a long time."

"That's okay Phylicia, I should have told you more about my condition before." Jack then told Phylicia the details of his illness. He found it easy to talk to her and ended up telling her the story of his past few years. It was the first time he had opened up to someone since Miri had died.

After he had finished Phylicia said, "Jack I just want you to know that I will help in whatever way I can, even if you just need someone to talk to."

"Thanks Phylicia. I appreciate your concern, and I will let you know if there is anything you can do."

They talked a bit more before Phylicia had to get back to her office. Jack returned to his apartment.

It was the following evening that he got an email from the university research committee. It informed him that his research had been suspended. That it was the property of the university, and that he should not use or claim any of the results as his own. And that Jack had been taken off the roll of Ph.D. candidates. If he should wish to renew his application for Ph.D., he would need to reapply with the proper forms. The email wished him well and mentioned that official paperwork would follow.

At first, he was a bit stunned at the bluntness and speed with which the committee had seemed to make its decision. After talking to Professor Camble he expected a more tactful approach to be taken. But he knew how competitive research positions had become in the past few years, especially following the employment crisis.

Though young at the time Jack remembered that the crisis had started as the automation of jobs became more common in the developed world. Transportation was automated, jobs were lost. Fast-food was automated, jobs were lost. Retail was automated, jobs were lost. By the time automation spread into the developing world, the crisis was too visible for governments to dismiss it. To quell the rising unrest, governments all over the world had no choice but to establish a guaranteed lifetime income. The income was to be paid by a tax on automation, a tax to which businesses vociferously objected, but became resigned to pay as they realized that without purchasing power, people simply couldn't buy the goods the now automated businesses produced.

Conservative pundits predicted that a government-provided life-income would lead to a majority of the population spending their time in virtual pursuits such as gaming. And while a lot of people did spend their days in virtual worlds others, feeling liberated from the immediate need to earn a living, were pursuing learning and advanced degrees as an outlet for their energies. This had created a huge demand for positions in undergraduate and graduate programs. Universities found they could pick and choose the students they admitted to their programs.

By the time Jack entered graduate school many disciplines

had stiff competition for admittance and continued enrollment. He had seen others lose their positions in labs because they were deemed not to be serious enough about their research. Or because they hadn't put the hours in, or because they had questioned their assignments, or they had questioned their adviser's motives. Anyone that didn't show complete devotion was subject to immediate dismissal without recourse. Jack knew he wasn't unique.

It was decided then, he thought. He went out for a walk.

His Annie alerted as he reentered his apartment. It was Phylicia. "Hi Jack, this is Phylicia. I was just calling because I heard what happened with your research."

"You found out already?"

"Well, I was in the lab when they buttoned up your experiment, which I found disturbing, so I started asking around. I guess I've developed some good sources over the years; it didn't take long to find out what was going on."

"Then you know that I've not only lost control of my experiment; I've also lost my standing in the doctorate program, and any use of the results of my research."

"They kicked you out of the program too? I didn't know that. I don't understand, I mean how could they do that?"

"Supposedly it is in the agreement we signed when we entered the Ph.D. program. If for any reason we abandon our research, we can be required to forfeit our place in the program. The research committee claims that my request for a six-month sabbatical constitutes abandonment. But I guess it's to be expected, you know how competitive research positions are today. I wouldn't be surprised if they don't replace us all with research Annies."

"Jack that is so unfair! They just want to get their hands on your research, that's what I think."

"I've been thinking I haven't made as much progress as I should have and besides," Jack paused, her words sinking in.

"Why do you think that someone is trying to appropriate my research?"

"Because, no matter what you say, you've made more progress than all the others. There is a lot of jealousy in that lab. Someone has decided to take this opportunity to steal your research."

"Do you think steal is the right word?"

"I'm afraid it is the right word. That is the state of university research these days. Did you know that most of the research done in that lab can't even be reproduced? I've tried and I for one question their results. I wouldn't be surprised if Kenneth doesn't take over your research, he's always been Professor Camble's favorite and Camble is under pressure from the administration to show some results out of his lab. That's probably why he didn't stand up for you."

"Well, I don't like to think of science being practiced like that, but you may be right, I've seen others treated not much better. I will just have to do what I can to keep my research alive while I recuperate."

"Jack, if you need anything from the lab or the university just call. I'll be glad to help you with any research you pursue."

CHAPTER 7

The long flight from LAX to Guangzhou, China was over. Now it was only another hour until landing at Tang Son Nhat International Airport in Ho Chi Minh City.

Dr. Roberta Hughes of the CDC was going to Vietnam to investigate a viral outbreak in the western part of southern Vietnam. The virus seemed highly contagious but not life-threatening. Out of the hundreds of cases Vietnam health authorities were monitoring, only one person had died.

That was different from the virus outbreak that her colleague Dr. Williams had investigated in South Sudan the month before. There the virus was highly virulent but not so contagious. Unfortunately, he had lost his samples trying to leave the country during a tribal uprising and apparently the virus had run its course, so the CDC had not been able to make a definitive classification except for what Dr. Williams' Annie had analyzed.

Dr. Hughes drifted off to sleep and was awakened by one of the flight attendants upon landing. The entire trip had taken nearly thirty hours including layovers.

In the modern terminal, Dr. Hughes saw someone holding up a sign with her name on it. The person turned out to be Dr. Cam Nguyen.

"Hello, I'm Roberta Hughes."

"Hello, I am Cam Nguyen. I work with the Health Ministry and will be your guide during your stay in Vietnam. I hope you had a pleasant flight?"

"Yes, too long, but overall, not a bad flight."

"Good, let us get you through immigration and then pick up your luggage downstairs."

With the help of Cam, it didn't take long to be processed through immigration. Dr. Hughes had her passport and visa in order. Baggage claim was typical of any large airport, harried but workable.

Dr. Hughes had nothing to declare in customs, and she and

Cam passed on through and out of the terminal. Dr. Nguyen looked to her left and waved, a small SUV started toward them. The driver loaded Dr. Hughes's luggage, and they were on their way to the hotel that Cam had booked for Dr. Hughes. Coming out of the terminal it was only a short drive-up Bach Dang to the Palm Hotel.

It was late afternoon and Dr. Hughes remarked how busy the streets were, with cars and SUVs and the ubiquitous motorbikes passing on the right.

"Yes," said Dr. Nguyen. "And this is as light as the traffic gets today, I'm afraid."

After making sure Roberta was checked into her room Dr. Nguyen said good night and that they would start for Chau Doc early in the morning.

Roberta ate some dinner in her room and studied the reports Cam had given her. Chau Doc was a fishing village on the Hau River in An Giang province, close to the Cambodia border. It seemed to be the epicenter of the breakout. Three-hundred and fifty-three people had been infected so far with still only one death. The CDC had been called in at the request of the World Health Organization (WHO) which the Vietnamese had appealed to. So technically Roberta was there representing WHO and not the CDC, but she really didn't care for the fine politics. She was just intent on getting samples and field intelligence and getting back to the CDC for analysis. She put the reports back in her bag and went to bed.

Early the next morning Roberta and Cam were on the road with their driver Huynh Hoang. Roberta noticed the driver was completely quiet though apparently competent.

"The traffic is incredible," remarked Dr. Hughes. "Is it always this bad?"

"This is typical for a morning rush hour," said Dr. Nguyen. "We should make better time once we clear Ho Chi Minh outskirts. It shouldn't take more than four or five hours to drive to Chau Doc."

"I have to say that Ho Chi Minh City is quite modern and

beautiful. I really didn't know what to expect but thought it would be much older. What will Chau Doc be like?"

"Yes, Ho Chi Minh has changed much in the last couple of decades. Very much development and very much population increase. Much of the old city has been redeveloped except the outskirts. Now Chau Doc is a much smaller city. It has only a population of about one-hundred fifty thousand. The Hau River flows through town to the Mekong. The floating city, houseboats as you would say, is quite famous. It is also excellent for fish and sauces. We will try them tonight?"

"Sounds good," said Roberta.

Roberta and Cam talked most of the way to Chau Doc, discussing their professional careers and educational experiences and the current viral outbreak. As they talked Roberta noticed the changing scenery. From city to town to more rural. She noticed the houses became fewer but still were located close to the road with fields stretching out far behind. She also noticed that while the roads ran very straight, they had to turn many times to apparently make their way to the few bridges that crossed the many watercourses between Ho Chi Minh City and Chau Doc.

It was eleven-thirty in the morning when the SUV pulled into the Victoria Chau Doc Hotel. After lunch at the hotel, the driver dropped off Roberta and Cam at the Binh An Hospital where they went on rounds with the hospital's Medical Director. Roberta took notes and made pictures with her Annie. Blood samples were provided by the hospital personnel in a small sample satchel. Roberta did not bother to analyze these with her Annie as she could do a much more thorough job at the CDC in a couple of days. It was late in the day when they arrived back at the Victoria.

"We will go to dinner in thirty minutes; I will take you to the floating cafe?" asked Cam.

"Yes, I'll meet you in the lobby."

They arrived at what appeared to be a floating barge, the sign said Con Tien Restaurant. The driver dropped them off; Dr. Nguyen arranged for him to be available by phone. They were seated on the upper level which was open to the air with a curved roof above.

The menu was mostly fish or chicken served with a selection of Vietnamese fish sauces. Roberta chose fish, Cam had chicken. Several fish sauces came with the meal including 'Red Boat' which became Roberta's favorite.

“This is excellent,” said Roberta.

“I'm so glad you like it,” said Cam. “As you can taste it's very important to find a fish sauce you like to highlight the meal.”

They spent their dinner mostly discussing the viral outbreak. When they had finished their meals, Cam called the driver while she and Roberta drank a glass of wine. The drive back to the hotel was uneventful. Roberta was soon asleep.

She knew something was wrong as soon as she awoke the next morning.

CHAPTER 8

After the shock of losing his research wore off, Jack started to think about his future. He was determined not to give up on his goal of a cure for viral infections. But he would have to redirect his efforts into something like software design and simulation, something he could afford since he no longer had access to a well-stocked biology lab. He could do a few simple DIY tests on his synthetic biology constructs, but most of the in-depth lab work and testing would be done by others, he hoped.

Jack felt confident his virus detection circuit would have worked. So, his first step would be to program and simulate such a circuit using standard synthetic biology components.

Next, he would pursue an idea that had occurred to him about how to stop a viral infection. He knew that one way the human body responded to a virus was by generating antibodies that mimicked cellular receptors and would bind to the virus-associated protein (VAP) of the virion (a viral package before cell infection). With all its binding sites occupied, the virion was effectively prevented from anchoring itself to a cell and causing infection.

Jack believed he could do something similar by creating what he called blocking molecules. These would mimic the cellular receptors and attach themselves to a virion's VAPs and neutralize the virus.

Once his virus detector identified the virus-associated protein, he would use genetic tools to assemble DNA snippets into blocking molecules for that VAP. The current strategy of developing such molecules was quite expensive because of its trial-and-error aspects. Jack hoped that his design-oriented approach would reduce the cost significantly.

The delivery vehicle to get his virus neutralizers into the human body would be similar to the branching molecules called dendrimers. These were symmetrical three-dimensional self-assembling molecules. They currently served as excellent spherical 'cages' to deliver RNA and DNA into cells. Jack reasoned he could build upon the software that he had written for the design of three-dimensional integrated circuits to build his dendrimer inspired delivery cages, d-cages, as he came to call them.

Finally, he would use the techniques of ANI available as a package through one of the cloud providers to make the software smart. The ANI would be able to help researchers set up and interpret the software solutions. Once trained, it would also be able to offer ideas for further investigation to the researchers.

All he needed was access to a synthetic biology component database, an ANI cloud provider, and support for publishing his software. And Jack thought he knew someone who could help.

He called Phylicia and told her what he needed. As expected, she had a contact in the IT department at the university; give her a few minutes she said, and she would find out what resources were available. She hung up.

A few minutes later, Jack's Annie announced a caller. "Hi Jack, this is Phylicia. Here is what I have found. My friend tells me we could use the university's 'Open Access Program' to request the use of university computer resources. The program is ostensibly a public outreach program that was designed to encourage high school students with their science projects, but there have been cases where others were also allowed into the program. My friend assures me that your request is a proper fit for the program's objectives. She will put in the necessary paperwork and let us know when it's available."

"Wow, that is great Phylicia; you really came through. I think that deserves at least a dinner; what do you say?"

"Well, I didn't do it for a reward, but a dinner would be nice, thanks."

"Okay, I'll call you soon, thanks again."

"Um, okay Jack, bye."

CHAPTER 9

Roberta definitely felt something was wrong. Her head was pounding, and her mouth was very dry. Her eyes itched, almost burning in intensity. She quickly showered and dressed. By the time she called Cam's Annie, she felt feverish.

"Good morning, Cam, this is Roberta. I'm sorry to be calling so early, but I'm not feeling very well. I was wondering if you could come to my room?"

"I'll be there as soon as I can get dressed."

Roberta put the few things she had into her bags so that she would be prepared to leave. She then lay back down on the bed to wait for Cam. She was sure she had a fever. There was a knock at the door.

Roberta opened the door to let Cam in. "That was fast," she said.

"So, you feel bad. Have you used your Annie to check your vitals?"

"No. Funny but I hadn't thought about it. It's in my bag there."

A minute of silence passed as Cam used Roberta's Annie to check her vitals. "Temperature one hundred," said Cam. "You definitely have a fever. Heart rate elevated, blood pressure elevated. Are there any other symptoms you've noticed?"

"Yes," said Roberta. "I have a headache and my eyes are burning."

"But no nausea?"

"No, not yet anyway."

"Okay," said Cam, putting the Annie back in Roberta's bag. "Let's get out of here and on our way to Ho Chi Minh. I want Dr. Dao to check you."

Cam called the driver, explaining that Dr. Hughes wasn't feeling well and they needed to leave immediately.

"What is wrong with her?" asked the driver.

"I don't know. Could be just a little food poisoning, but we need to get her back to Ho Chi Minh as soon as possible."

"Yes," said the driver. "Okay, I'll be there in twenty minutes."

Roberta and Cam were waiting outside the hotel; the dawn was just breaking when the driver drove up. He quickly put the bags in the vehicle, all the time watching Roberta. As Cam started to help Roberta into the SUV, she suddenly became limp and collapsed to the sidewalk.

"Help me!" yelled Cam.

The driver looked around from the back of the vehicle and saw Roberta on the sidewalk. Instead of moving to assist Cam, he turned and ran the other way. He was in the SUV and racing away before Cam knew what had happened.

A guest of the hotel came out and assisted Cam in getting Roberta back inside. By this time, Roberta had recovered from her faint. A hotel staff member started assisting Roberta, and this allowed Cam to call the Health Ministry back in Ho Chi Minh.

After finishing her call, Cam came back to Roberta.

“How are you feeling, Roberta?”

“I'm better, though my head is still throbbing.”

“You probably missed it, but the driver took off. I think when he saw you faint it scared him into thinking you might have the Chau Doc virus. Anyway, I've called the ministry, and they've agreed to send a plane to pick us up at the local airport. They should be here in a little over an hour. Do you think you can make it?”

“I'll be okay. As long as I can sit down while waiting.”

The hotel arranged for one of their employees to drive Roberta and Cam to the local airport.

Sitting in the airport waiting on the plane, Roberta started drifting in and out of consciousness and talking nonsense to Cam.

“Aunt Lucy will be here anytime Kimmy,” said Roberta. “We should just wait here; mom won't like it if we wander off.”

Cam was disturbed but played along. “Okay Roberta, we'll

wait here." This is moving fast, thought Cam. I have to get her to the hospital and soon.

Roberta had fallen into a fitful sleep by the time the plane arrived. A stretcher was brought into the airport waiting area, and Roberta was carried onto the plane by a couple of orderlies. Dr. Dao was waiting and started an IV immediately. Cam was relieved to see the doctor.

"Oh, thank you, Dr. Dao, for coming. I was really getting worried; her fever is very high, and she started hallucinating and then became listless and unresponsive."

"You've done well Dr. Nguyen. I'm hopeful that the IV will help her and we will be able to get her back to the hospital where we can further treat her. It certainly appears that she has caught the infection she was sent here to study. How ironic."

Roberta spent a week in the hospital intensive care and then another week in a private room before recovering. After a week of staying with Cam at her apartment, she was scheduled to fly back to the States. She would meet someone from the CDC at the airport to assist her if needed.

The driver and SUV had still not turned up so Roberta had nothing to take with her to the airport. She only had the new clothes that Cam had bought for her that week. She had her papers replaced by the American Embassy in Ho Chi Minh with the Vietnamese government helping with the red tape. Cam promised to send new samples to her as soon as possible, but Roberta still felt dejected about losing the first batch.

As they were finishing at immigration, Roberta saw someone she recognized in the crowd. It was Wesley Williams. Wesley ran up to Roberta and hugged her.

"You don't look sick at all," said Wesley.

"I'm sure glad to see you, Wesley. Let me introduce you to Dr. Cam Nguyen; she's the reason I'm doing as well as I am."

Wesley and Cam shared greetings. Then Wesley said they should get on board the plane.

Roberta and Cam hugged, and Roberta said how grateful she was to Cam for all that she had done.

As they sat down in their seats on the plane, Roberta turned to Wesley and said, “I lost everything Wesley, my samples, my Annie, everything."

She seemed about to cry when Wesley said, “Well, the important thing is that we still have you.”

“That's kind Wesley, but I feel like such a failure.”

“No, you don't understand what I mean, and I thought you were supposed to be the smart one,” he smiled. “We have you and the antibodies in your blood. You see, we have everything we need to ID this virus.”

“You're right Wesley. I've been so despondent I haven't been thinking straight. You're right,” she smiled.

CHAPTER 10

Jack began working to the exclusion of all else, even forgetting the dinner he had promised Phylicia. But Phylicia didn't forget Jack, she helped him move to a cheaper apartment and continued to check in with him and even contributed some of her expertise to his research.

He worked for weeks programming and simulating his virus detection idea. When finished, he put the resultant software, V-Detect, up on the web site.

Next, he started modifying his old IC software to build his delivery vehicle, d-cages. Research in a corner of science called foldamers (self-assembling molecular folding structures) was helpful with this step.

His approach proposed to use two spherical cages, one inside the other. The outer cage would be covered in virus detectors. Once attached to a virus the cage would exactly mimic the topology of the virus. The synthetic biology tool would then identify the virus-associated protein and create a program for the blocking molecules.

Inside the inner cage DNA snippets (held there so that they could be protected from the identification tools of the outer cage) would be assembled according to the program created by the synthetic biology tool until the blocking molecule was complete. When finished the blocking molecule would be released into the body.

Unlike integrated circuits, his d-cages would self-organize. He would have to add to the software so that the primary structure, the arrangement of atomic composition and chemical bonds needed for the desired result, could be predicted. Then he would add simulation of the self-assembly of the cage in different solvent baths and extract the resulting size parameters.

It was a few more weeks until he first put the software, D-

Cages, up on the website provided by the school.

Next, he integrated his software with the ANI cloud expert provided by the university. This consisted mostly of running many design iterations and training the ANI until it could propose, set up and run its own designs. Surprisingly this took more time than anything else.

Finally, with the help of Phylicia, he put up his proposal for the DNA assembly of the blocking molecules. This part of the design was necessarily the sketchiest as Jack had never been able to test any of its ideas.

When finished, Jack decided to promote his site. He posted announcements to all the biology magazines that had an online presence and an open blog. Finally, he made the announcement on a biocoder blog page, a page that a lot of the DIY biology community outside academia and some academics frequented.

He hoped that his open software approach would attract researchers with whom he could establish a relationship and maybe encourage them to pursue his complete program. The response was encouraging, especially from the biocoder community, which led to his next problem.

CHAPTER 11

Jack's return visits to the doctor were going well. The gene therapy had repaired the damage caused by the mini-stroke and all the tests pointed to complete recovery. The doctor noted that Jack seemed more relaxed and cheerful. Jack agreed, he had also noticed he had more energy and was enjoying his work again. The reward of doing the job his way and the interaction and thanks he received from other researchers made the hours fly. He was focused and much more able to take things in stride, a trait he would soon find useful.

Jack was awakened early one morning a few weeks after he had posted his software by a call. It was from Phylicia. “Jack, we have a problem,” she said.

“Oh, hi Phylicia what's up,” he said sleepily.

“Your website, access is above normal, my friend tells me it's under investigation by the administration. She doesn't know how much longer it will be allowed to remain online.”

“Phylicia the website can't go down now, it is making a significant contribution to the independent research community.”

“I know Jack, I’m sorry.”

“Isn't there some way to placate the administrators?”

“Well, according to my friend they are going to want to meet the 'high school student' who created it. What are we going to do?”

“First, tell your friend that I’m sorry for the trouble. I'm also sorry I got you involved in this; I never expected there to be so much interest in the software. I thought it would take months not weeks before I made any headway with the research community. Second, tell your friend to give the administration my name and phone number, I'll explain as best I can. And I'll do my best to minimize the involvement of anyone else.”

“Okay Jack. I'll keep you informed, and don’t worry about me I can take care of myself, bye.”

Things moved fast, less than a week later a meeting had been scheduled between Jack and the university administrators. Jack knew that he needed to present a convincing case that would persuade the administrators to fund the website for the good of the research community.

When Jack had finished his presentation the university's Head of Information Technology spoke up, "Mr. Jackson we are not here to argue the worth of your research. But that you have used the resources of this university in a somewhat deceptive way I believe can also not be argued. You have used a public outreach program set up by the university to encourage high school students with their research and you have used it for personal reasons. We understand that your proposal passed our committee's approval, but this website on our server is supporting researchers without recognition of the university's resources being used. We also believe that your promotion of some discredited methods of synthetic biology reflects poorly on the university. We think we have been very understanding so far. But because of the reasons I have just stated, we must now advise you that you have one week to move your website to other servers or we will be forced to shut it down without your cooperation. Do you understand Mr. Jackson?"

Jack felt defeated. "Yes," he said.

Back in his apartment Jack posted that the website would need a new home and that he only had a week to find one. He received words of encouragement from the researchers using his software. Most of them weren't even involved in viral research but were using it for biological redesign, synthetic bio-bricks, and a host of other applications. But unfortunately, even with all the well wishes, no one offered him a host server.

Jack sighed.

Oh Miri, won't I ever learn?

CHAPTER 12

At first, it didn't seem like much of a problem. A few sailors returning from a six-month tour of duty in the Indian Ocean reporting to the hospital at Naval Station Norfolk in Virginia. Doctors begin cataloging their flu-like symptoms and treating them for a viral infection although they didn't know what virus was involved.

As a young child, Sal Jeremy had played with his father's old Navy hat. His father had worked his way up to ship's captain before he was killed in the Third Gulf War. Sal had determined early that he would join the Navy when he was old enough.

He had just returned from an Indian Ocean cruise and was looking forward to traveling home when he began to feel a little run down.

"Hey Milton," said Sal. "You want to go over to the base gym and workout a little?"

George Salton was called Milton because of his penchant to read poetry. "Sure," said George, "let's go."

The base gym was almost empty that morning. Sal and George worked adjacent treadmills for almost an hour. Suddenly Sal's knees buckled, he caught himself from falling.

"What's wrong Sal?" asked George. "Did you trip?"

Sal had stopped his treadmill and was leaning against the stand. "No, I just felt extremely weak for a moment."

"Maybe we better take a break," said George.

They walked over to the coffee bar and sat down. After a cup of coffee Sal said, "Milton I'm still not feeling right, maybe I should go see a doctor."

"Sure. Can you walk ok?"

"Yeah," said Sal.

George was walking beside Sal and conjecturing about all the things that might have caused Sal to feel sick. " … And that food we had last evening, I for one felt sick just looking at it, maybe that's the problem."

Just then Sal's knees started to buckle again, George caught him.

"Sal, Sal! What's wrong?"

Sal didn't answer, so George bent Sal's body over his shoulder and took off in a jog towards the hospital.

Besides Sal, others were being treated for the same symptoms, three were released within twenty-four hours. But Sal and the rest weren't responding to treatment. The medical personnel were becoming worried.

Thirty hours after George had brought Sal into the hospital, he was dead. George had called his family to tell them Sal had entered the hospital, Sal's commanding officer now called to give them the bad news.

The day after the first men had reported sick to the base hospital two dozen more men, including Sal, showed up. On the third day, another twenty men came in sick. The fourth day was more crowded with nearly forty men coming in. Within a week half the crew from that particular ship, nearly one hundred and seventy sailors had visited or were in the hospital. Then other sailors showed up that had not been on the stricken ship. By this time the death toll had risen to forty-five, with twice that number in serious condition.

There were some who died only hours after contracting the disease. The symptoms always started as a headache and burning eyes. If the infection continued to progress as Wesley Williams had witnessed in South Sudan months before, it would not be long until they started coughing up blood and then, gasping for air, they would drown in their own body fluids. The doctors tried everything, nothing helped. Whether it took hours or days the results were the same for more than fifty percent of the infected. But if they could survive more than a few days they almost always recovered.

The CDC was alerted and they sent a researcher, Dr. Hughes. She took samples that the Navy doctors had prepared back to her lab. There she discovered that they were dealing with a new strain of the flu that had been seen a few years before. It seemed also to have elements of the virus Wesley Williams had found in South Sudan and the influenza she had caught in Vietnam.

Roberta wondered if it could be a MGE (mobile genetic element) moving from one virus to the other. That would be a first, she thought, anyway a vaccine was needed and fast.

Almost immediately the entire medical establishment of the country was alerted to the problem. An effort to develop a vaccine was begun. A study of the possibility of an MGE being the genesis of the new virus was started. Field canvassing to find others infected began.

But even with the assurance from the medical community that a vaccine was imminent, the constant barrage of media reports and the memory of the last outbreak caused fear to grip the public.

Many movie houses, restaurants, shopping centers and other public spaces closed due to the fear of exposure to the flu. Government had declared martial law in some places. Face masks of doubtful efficacy were required by law for anyone venturing into public. In urban areas, National Guard troops accompanied morgue runs that picked up dead bodies. To maintain quarantine the government banned private burial services and instituted public burials, mass graves became common.

People that still worked tried to stay home and were living off what savings they had amassed. Those that didn't work were impacted when services provided by human workers began to fail. Robotic workers were able to make up some of the labor shortage. But even so, there was often a lack of needed public services.

Without shoppers, the commercial retail system struggled to continue functioning. The government began to make up for the faltering commercial systems. Automated convoys guarded by manned military vehicles moved food and other goods from producers to local distribution centers. Other troops accompanied the usual robotic delivery vans to see to it that the foodstuffs were distributed safely to local markets or homes. The government printed the money it needed to keep the system from collapsing although hyper-inflation was a worry.

People providing services the government considered essential that weren't yet provided by robots were drafted into the employ of their country. Essentials included food, transportation, law enforcement, energy, and network communications among others. Trade between countries started to fall as goods considered non-essential were allowed to sit in warehouses and factories. Network connections became the basis for staying in touch with relatives and friends.

Streets empty, routine interrupted, the mounting worry paralyzed entire nations. Only a few brave (or criminal) souls went out in public.

CHAPTER 13

Jose loved to ride his bicycle. He had wanted this particular model since he was six years old. He had worked hard to save money, taking out the trash, cleaning his room, and lately, keeping the yard robots in line. And now at the age of eleven, with the help of his dad, he had his bike. The only problem, he hadn't been able to ride it for the past few weeks. Because of the virus outbreak, his mom wouldn't let him leave the yard. He talked to his dad, but he told Jose to listen to his mom.

But this Saturday morning in Los Angeles while his mom and dad slept late, he was determined to take his bike out for a ride. He applied the tube of 'Secure Skin' his mother had bought to his arms and other exposed areas. 'Secure Skin' was a virus repellent made out of aligned carbon nanotube channels which were small enough to keep out viruses (and chemical agents) but still allow air molecules to pass. He sealed his helmet to his shirt with duct tape and spread 'Secure Skin' on that also. He carefully and quietly rolled the bicycle out the side door of the garage. He waited until he got to the end of the driveway before mounting and riding towards his school.

The built-in heads-up display of his helmet used GPS to show his location in relation to the surrounding streets. It also showed vehicles equipped with locators which were required by law during peacetime. He could focus on an area of the screen to ID the other traffic. The display was relatively quiet except for some vehicles near the school. He focused and the screen identified the vehicles as belonging to the west coast unit of Homeland Security, Urban Task Force. He would have to avoid the school.

Jose turned left on Manzanita Street. He would go down to North Hoover and take Burns Street. He was half-way down Burns Street when he saw some fast-approaching vehicles on the display. They would cross just ahead of him on North Virgil. Focusing, he found them to be Department of Defense troop transports. This would be cool, he thought. He would hide behind the parked SUV ahead and watch. He shut down his display.

The rumble increased, he felt the ground shaking, and a roar as the first vehicle passed. From his gameplay, he identified it as a robotic ground sweep. Its duty was to scout ahead of the convoy for any enemy activity, or in this case, cross-street traffic. As that roar settled down there came another roar and rumble as he saw troop transports passing. He counted ten transports each with a capacity of twenty troops. The rumble was just quietening when he heard a vehicle approaching. Another sweeper brought up the rear.

He was just about to arise when he heard the buzzing overhead. He ducked back down ending up flat on his back under the SUV. Skyward were robotic drones searching for movement below. He stayed as still as he could for as long as he could until he thought the drones must have moved on.

Jose got up slowly. Cool, he thought. He was just about to jump on his bike when the doors of the SUV flew open.

"What we got here, who you junior?" said a man. Two others also emerged from the SUV.

"I'm Jose, who wants to know?" said Jose defiantly, though he was backing away and looking for a way out.

The man laughed and said, "Who wants to know? I'll tell you shrimp, I wants to know. Me and my friends wants to know. We wants to know if you carrying any money?"

Jose had ten dollars in his pocket. "No, who you think I am, a Rockefella?"

The man laughed again, "You're a funny kid, gonna be a shame messing you up." He lunged at Jose.

Jose spun ninety degrees to the charging man and started to run mounting his bike on the fly.

He jumped the sidewalk on the other side and headed for the alley between buildings. Except it wasn't really an alley more like a narrow opening. Jose moved his hands in on the handlebars to avoid having them scrap the bricks on either side. He heard the men yelling behind him and the SUV starting.

Jose popped into the open and turned sharply left onto a narrow parking lot. He heard the screech of tires behind him as he made it to the end of the lot. Darting to the right under a tree and onto a lawn, Jose didn't slow down.

He emerged onto another parking lot and once past an open gate turned left on the sidewalk of Normal Avenue. Jose began looking for another open gate and made an almost immediate left between some low buildings. He zig-zagged his way back north to Burns, not slowing until he got to the sidewalk.

He carefully peddled to the corner of Burns and N. Virgil where the SUV had been parked on the other side of the street. His heads-up showed no traffic on Burns or N. Virgil, but it could be the SUV was blocking its signal. He stopped and pushed his bike to the corner of the building and looked slowly up and down N. Virgil. Seeing no vehicles he took off in a hurry crossing N. Virgil and flying down Burns.

His heads-up showed no traffic on the cross-street Madison, so he blew through the intersection without slowing down. He turned left on N. Vermont Avenue and was soon at his destination, Osteen Drugs.

Jose had met the owner, Jason Osteen, at the cafe on the corner where Jose liked to buy milkshakes. Jason was reading the same old-school comic as Jose except in paper. Jose couldn't believe that such an old guy would be reading the same comic and a paper comic at that. They got to talking and Jason suggested to Jose that he should come over to the store and see Jason's collection of paper comics. Anytime he wanted he could pick out a comic and take it home to read. Jose had been going there every few weeks since.

Jose noticed the yellow ribbon across the entrance to the store. He tried the door, but it was locked. The glass in the door had been broken and plywood covered the opening. Jose looked up and down the street, for the first time he felt the strangeness of the outbreak, it wasn't just news on the TV now. Jose felt a shiver; he turned his bike and headed back home as fast as he could.

CHAPTER 14

One evening as Jack was still searching for a host for his website there was a knock at the door.

It was Phylicia, and she had been crying. "Hi Phylicia, come in, what's the matter?"

"I've been suspended from the lab. Professor Camble said I had been using my time in an unauthorized manner; I guess he means the time I've devoted to your project."

"I'm so sorry Phylicia. I can't believe this is happening to you. Just because you were trying to help me."

"It's those non-disclosure agreements we signed, they are written in such a way that we are nothing but slaves to the university, we haven't rights to anything."

"This is my fault Phylicia. I shouldn't have allowed you to get involved. I've been foolish to think that the university is something other than a business. That they were interested in furthering knowledge in whatsoever way possible. All they are interested in is money and notoriety."

"I wouldn't be surprised if Camble hadn't encouraged the university to shut down your site," she said.

"You might be right Phylicia but it's out of our hands now. With this viral outbreak and the general state of the world we can't be concerned with the machinations of the university anymore. We have to do the things necessary to take care of ourselves and help others."

He continued, "And right now I think the only thing we can do is have that dinner I promised you long ago. I think we could both use a quiet evening. How about it, I'll cook us some food?"

"Sure, Jack that would be nice."

As they sat down to eat Jack offered up a prayer before they began, something he hadn't done since he was a young man.

Jack had taken Phylicia home late that night, as they had talked well into the evening. It was Saturday morning and he was still in bed when his Annie announced a call from a Dr. Roberta Hughes. Dr. Hughes introduced herself as a researcher in the Infectious Diseases Pathology Branch of the Centers for Disease Control and Prevention, she had been one of those using Jack's software. After telling Jack how great a help his software, especially D-Cages, had been to her research, she began to impress upon him the need to get his site back up and soon when Jack interrupted and asked, "Excuse me Dr. Hughes, but why do you think it is so urgent?"

"Mr. Jackson we at the CDC believe we have a real problem. The plague virus of a few years ago seems to be back and it appears to be more contagious than before. I don't have to tell you what that could mean."

"No," said Jack coldly. "You don't, I know what that could mean."

"Yes, and I believe that only the combination of services your site provided will help us with the virus detection and delivery mechanism modeling my lab needs to do in time to save lives. We have a vaccine already in development but of course, that only protects those not yet infected."

"Well, the biggest problem I face right now in re-establishing the site is that I don't have a host server and cloud ANI. And I don't have the money to lease them."

"I think the CDC can help you with that Mr. Jackson."

"You mean you will provide support free of charge?"

"Yes, we can provide you with the necessary space in our cloud and ANI access if you will commit to getting it set up and online. Mr. Jackson, I guarantee the CDC will be willing to take care of everything else."

"Alright Dr. Hughes, I'll do what I can to get it set up as soon as possible."

"Thank you, Mr. Jackson and good luck. I will have someone contact you with the information you will need."

Jack called Phylicia. "Guess what," he said when Phylicia answered.

“What is it, Jack?”

“I've just finished talking to Dr. Roberta Hughes with the CDC. They want me to get the website set up again. And you'll never believe it. They are offering to provide the servers and any other support I need.”

“Jack that's great. But I wonder why?”

“Well, there is a serious reason for their offer. They think the global viral epidemic of a few years ago is back and some of the researchers involved in its investigation were using the site previously and believe it would be an asset to have it up and running again.”

“That's wonderful. I mean your work could really make a difference in people's lives, just as you wanted.”

“You're right Phylicia, I hadn't thought about it but that is what it is really about, making a difference. But you got one thing wrong.”

“What is it Jack?”

“It's our work now, not just mine.”

CHAPTER 15

Of course, there were those who tried to take every advantage of the situation. They stole what they could and sold it on the black market. They promised cures for a price that some desperate families could not resist when faced with the loss of a loved one. Perhaps the worst of the worst were those that threatened to infect people if they did not pay the price the extortioners demanded. These were the most sought after by law enforcement. Pervasive surveillance and biometrics proved their worth as arrests were eventually made.

But no matter how hard the government tried there were always people falling through the safety net. Then something happened that was unexpected. Private individuals took it upon themselves to deliver services to those in need. It wasn't just altruism though; it was as commercial as any business. But except for a few outliers, most of the services were provided at a reasonable cost considering the danger the providers were taking upon themselves. It was enough to supplement the government's efforts and keep those in need from perishing. It was enough to keep some semblance of order in a society on the brink of disintegration.

But it wasn't enough to keep complete order.

"Damn kid!" exclaimed Rivera, pounding the steering wheel.

"Okay," he said to the other two, Lamoille and Camel. "We've wasted enough time, what's the next address Camel?"

"765 Hyperion Avenue," said Camel.

The SUV pulled into the driveway and stopped. The driveway continued to the back of the house. The house itself had at one time been a single private residence, maybe a hundred years old, it was now partitioned into separate units. The unit Rivera wanted was in the front.

Rivera unfolded his Annie and reviewed the target information. He then straightened his suit tie and walked up to the front door with the medical satchel in his hand. He knocked and waited.

An elderly lady called from inside, “Who is it?”

“Mrs. Cheevers?”

“Yes.”

“It's Dr. Joseph Sachs. If you remember, we talked over the phone?”

“Oh yes Dr. Sachs, I remember.”

“Mrs. Cheevers, I believe I told you I would try to get by today. Is it okay if I come in?”

“Well, I guess so, although I had forgotten it was today, wait while I get my keys.”

Once inside Rivera asked, “How is your husband today Mrs. Cheevers?”

“He sleeps most of the time. I don't think there is much change.”

“Have you considered what we discussed over the phone? I believe he is an excellent candidate for our treatment. I mean, as I told you, I can't guarantee it because each person reacts somewhat differently to the regimen but after our discussion, I believe he may be one of them.”

“Well, the doctors at the hospital aren't any more help. They've given up on poor Mitch. Do you really think it could do some good?”

“I wouldn't be here if I didn't think there was a good chance Mrs. Cheevers. I have to choose the patients carefully, there's only so many hours in the day.”

“Oh, I understand Dr. Sachs. It's just that it's a lot of money.”

“I know Mrs. Cheevers and I'm sorry to have to ask but your payment will go towards making more treatments that will be offered to others. For them, like your husband, it may be the only hope.”

“Okay Dr. Sachs, if you will administer your treatment I will get the checkbook. Is a check okay?”

“That will be fine Mrs. Cheevers.”

It didn't take Rivera long to administer the 'treatment', a concentrated vitamin B shot and leave the sugar pills with Mrs. Cheevers. He took the thousand-dollar check with him.

“Please keep me informed Mrs. Cheevers, you have my number, I am always available to my patients.”

“Thank you, Dr. Sachs and goodbye.”

“Goodbye Mrs. Cheevers.”

Back in the SUV, Rivera handed the check to Laimoille.

“Scan that quickly and make sure it deposits,” he said.

Laimoille scanned the check with his Annie. A few seconds and he signaled thumbs up. Rivera started the SUV.

“Who's next Camel?”

They drove away to their next 'appointment'.

CHAPTER 16

After a day and night of non-stop work, Jack and Phylicia almost had the site back up. The cloud servers the government provided were adequate but as with everything the government does there was a lot of resistance when doing even the simplest things. The security requirements were extremely confining, often stumping them until they could contact their CDC liaison who would then chase the request up the chain of command until he found a person that could resolve the problem.

Eventually, they had it all put together and brought the site up. By that time the flu epidemic had reached its peak.

Except for a few trips to see each other Jack and Phylicia had mostly stayed in their apartments after bringing the site up. For weeks they maintained and updated the software and site remotely. But now they had been invited to a meeting at the CDC by Dr. Hughes. Jack called Phylicia about the invitation. Because it would require them to fly, neither was looking forward to the trip. Still, they prepared for travel with a feeling of excitement.

Their first long-range venture outside their apartments since the epidemic had begun shocked them with what they saw. Streets deserted of people, except for troops and automated delivery vans. Checkpoints that had to be negotiated. Robotic drones overhead and robot security on foot. Barricades and barriers seemingly everywhere, nothing they had seen on television could compare with what they were seeing with their own eyes.

At one point Jack took Phylicia's hand absentmindedly.

"Jack?"

"Yes Phylicia."

"This is frightening, isn't it?"

"Yeah, that pretty much sums it up. It's amazing how fragile is civilization. Normality gone in a moment. I'm thinking I may be more afraid of the measures taken to meet this emergency than by the cause of the emergency itself."

They continued their ride to the airport quietly, taking in the strangeness of the scene, still holding hands.

At the airport, the old security was back, a thing they had only heard about. Besides checking ID's and tickets, security also scanned them for their temperature before allowing them to board the plane. At least the plane was only half full, the seat next to them was empty, no doubt a result of the viral outbreak.

Even though he had been there before Jack found Atlanta to be as strangely unfamiliar as Boston. It was as if the cities had been transported in total to a foreign country or a different planet. The enormity of the situation was more real to Jack now than it had ever been. He was glad he had been of help to the researchers at the meeting. He was glad Phylicia was with him.

The halls of the CDC were bustling with human researchers and robotic assistants. A robot concierge guided Jack and Phylicia to their seats.

The meeting began with introductions. It was an impressive assembly. Some of the better-known names were Dr. John Sailes of the National Institute of Allergy and Infectious Diseases at the National Institutes of Health, responsible for understanding how viruses were spread and how that might be prevented. Dr. Mary Heier, head of the Bureau of Biologics at the Food and Drug Administration, responsible for quality control and licensing of vaccines. Dr. James Gold of Virginia's Department of Public Health, the epicenter of the outbreak in the United States.

Dr. Frank Kilbourne, Director of the CDC, began the meeting.

"I want to thank everyone for being here today. We at the CDC have been tasked with spearheading the response to this influenza outbreak. As many of you know we could be seeing a new mutation mechanism with this virus where MGE is involved. But however it arose, we are pleased to report that researchers here at the CDC along with researchers at the

National Institutes of Health have produced a vaccine for this current strain. This is the fastest response ever to any viral outbreak. It was facilitated by the rapid increase in our ability to model and simulate the viral proteins and their delivery mechanism. We have already decided to have the vaccine mass-produced, and we want to thank those manufacturers who have responded to our call.

"We have also decided not to make this a mandatory inoculation but to allow local health authorities to decide the proper course to follow in their respective communities. We do however strongly recommend that everyone be vaccinated as soon as the vaccine becomes available, which should begin shipping in about two weeks, again a rapid response time by historical measures. We believe with the addition of this vaccine to our arsenal of treatments we will now be able to get ahead of the outbreak."

There was applause from the audience.

When it subsided Dr. Kilbourne continued, "We also want to announce an initiative to offer help to those who have already contracted the disease. As you know in any outbreak there are those that are already infected before they can be vaccinated. This highly contagious virus and its high rate of deaths have convinced us that we also need a way to treat those already infected and that we need to develop that treatment just as fast as we can. To that end, I have assigned Dr. Sydney Spencer, Deputy Director of the Office of Infectious Diseases here at the CDC to head the program. Sydney will now speak to you about this new initiative."

As Dr. Spencer was beginning to speak, a robot concierge came up to Jack and Phylicia and asked, "Are you Jack Jackson and Phylicia Hastings?"

"Yes," said Jack.

"Would you follow me please; I will take you to Dr. Hughes."

They were taken to the cafeteria and introduced to Dr. Hughes.

"Oh, Mr. Jackson, Ms. Hastings, I'm so pleased to meet you in person, call me Roberta please."

After asking Jack and Phylicia how they liked their coffee, Roberta turned to the robot concierge and asked that two more coffees be brought to the table.

"I hope you both are enjoying the conference. You two had much to do with making it possible you know."

"Yes, I do find it interesting, and please call me Jack. Although I have to admit, I'm not real sure why I was invited."

"We thought, that is I and my team, that you two would find it interesting to see what your work has allowed us here at the CDC to do and the researchers that have been using your software wanted to thank you both personally. I think you will be surprised how much your efforts have helped our research."

She continued, "It is no small thanks to you two that we were able to develop a vaccine for this infection. I would like to take you to meet some of my team."

"Thank you Roberta, we look forward to meeting them," said Jack.

After finishing their coffee Dr. Hughes took Jack and Phylicia to a lab room down one of the side corridors. Upon entering Jack saw about a dozen people. Dr. Hughes called for attention and introduced Jack and Phylicia to those assembled. Jack seemed embarrassed when several researchers congratulated him on his software, but Phylicia seemed pleased, if not for herself then for Jack.

Several of the researchers gathered around Jack and Phylicia in discussion.

"Mr. Jackson," said Mark Lindsey, one of the virologists.

"Please just call me Jack, Mr. Jackson is just too formal for me."

"Well Jack. Your software has been very helpful to my research and having an ANI link makes it even better to use. I was wondering what motivated you two to create such a great tool and make it open to all."

Jack related his original motivation to find a cure for the disease that had killed his family. He then told them about his health problems that had put that search on hold. He brought Phylicia into the conversation by saying how helpful she had been in the software's development and the price she had paid for that help.

Dr. Wesley Williams spoke up, "We've been able to apply your software to some of our existing projects and with good results. We are also interested in your program for research into providing a treatment for people already infected with a virus. I've been personally charged by Dr. Hughes to look into your idea of blocking molecules. As you know your idea is very similar to one of the ways the human body already employs to neutralize viruses. Have you made any more progress since your last posting?"

"No," said Jack. "I've given it a great deal of thought though. I don't see any reason the approach wouldn't work except for one thing."

"What is that?"

"I'm not sure the replication rate for the blocking molecules will be fast enough to block all the virions. It would basically be a race between the blocking molecule production rate and the virus reproduction rate."

"Yes," said Dr. Williams. "I had just about come to that conclusion myself. Do you have any ideas?"

"Well, the only way I see that we can be sure to get the production rates necessary is to use the body's cells themselves."

"You mean as the virus does? Infect cells with blocking molecule machinery and allow them to create the needed copies?"

"Yes."

"Preposterous," said one of the virologists listening. "But it might work."

"Jack," said Dr. Williams. "I hope you will consider collaborating with us as we pursue a viral cure."

"Certainly. I would be more than pleased to help out."

"Jack, Phylicia," said Dr. Hughes interrupting the discussion. "You may not realize exactly what you have done. You have essentially legitimized the use of synthetic biology in biological research. Something that, as you know, was frowned upon for years by the biology establishment because of the accident that killed the fruit flies."

"Well," said Jack. "I was an engineering student before I switched to biology so the idea of using synthetic biology to design a mechanism for viral detection seemed logical. The history of the reaction to that accidental release of gene drives from the Moscow lab seemed to me more of a knee jerk reaction among those fearful of foreign research groups. Gene drives, which everyone knows override natural selection to pass a desired trait down through succeeding generations, in this case, selection for male offspring only, have nothing to do with synthetic biology. As far as I know the reaction, which was never an outright ban, chilled synthetic biology research in academic labs here but nowhere else in the world which is probably why many people are looking at restarting their programs and why I continued with it in my research."

"I think you will find most of the researchers here at the CDC agree with you. But since we work for the government, we could not approach its use logically as you have," said a virologist.

"Well, I guess that is the result of not having a real job over the past few months and not needing official approval for my work. I am fortunate in what happened to me although at the time I was pretty distressed. I had personally wanted to be the one that discovered an effective approach to handling viral infections. You only realize after long reflection that it is the effort you contribute to the goal that counts not whatsoever you do."

"I would be willing to bet," said Dr. Hughes, "that the

methodology that you have provided for researchers here will eventually lead us to accomplishing the goal you set for yourself all those years ago, a universal viral cure."

"Thank you Roberta, those are kind words," said Jack.

"And you should be proud," continued Dr. Hughes, "of what you have accomplished so far. You have contributed just as much to helping us find a vaccine for this current outbreak as anyone here."

There was immediate agreement expressed by the other researchers.

"And I believe your wife and son would be proud too," said Phylicia.

Jack looked at Phylicia, he was smiling again.

LOOKING BACK

As I edit this novelette in 2026, I'm struck by a few items. This is one of the first stories I wrote at the end of 2016. I'm an electronic design engineer by training and my knowledge of biology is minimal. The fact I chose to write a story where biology is central is surprising now (I have a degree in physics).

I think it was motivated by reading some popular science articles about the future possibilities of synthetic biology. The mechanics of synthetic biology, where scientists take pre-built components and put them together in a new configuration and function, seemed similar to my work. I take components, ICs, resistors, capacitors, etc., and put them together for new functions.

My description of the outbreak and its effects, while not accurate in every way, does seem to recall the COVID era reaction of people and the government.

The idea of using synthetic biology to create new biological functions was reinforced recently by the engineering of a cell from components. As I understand it, the cell could divide for several generations, grow, and evolve to an extent. The scientist that created it denies that it is living, but it could eventually find usefulness in the manufacture of insulin, which is done by bacteria now, and maybe even the manufacture of plastics without oil, among other uses.

The characters in the story using a sample genome of the virus to build a "blocking molecule" and using software and ANI (artificial intelligence) seems a combination of mRNA techniques from the COVID era merged with the AI explosion of the past couple of years. But I used DNA which would be too dangerous to use in the real world. There even seems to be some issues with using the less dangerous mRNA vaccines.

When the main character Jack suggests that they use the

body's own cell machinery to make his “blocking molecule” in sufficient numbers to affect the viral infection, I couldn't help but think that something similar happened in my own body when I took the COVID vaccine.

Life imitates art, and art imitates life, I guess.

THANK YOU FOR READING

*Continue your journey to the stars with the next book of the 11 volume **From The Earth Series**:*

War Through The Pines

What starts in space may not stay in space. Many governments today are preparing for war in space. Most people today are unaware of it. When will it happen? How will it be conducted? What will be the effect on a young boy just coming of age?

Young Donner had already discovered a covert signal coming from the secret 'Battle Stars" in orbit before the war began.

Destruction of the Battle Stars begins the war which soon spreads to the Earth's surface and all the world.

See the author's website ***www.dwpatterson.com*** for availability and more information.

Hard Science Fiction – Old School.

THE FUTURE CHRON UNIVERSE

FROM THE EARTH SERIES:

The **From The Earth Series** consists of 10 novelettes and one novella. These are the foundational stories of the **Future Chron Universe**. They follow mankind's journey from Earth to the stars (or Alpha Centauri anyway). They are listed below in chronological order but may be read in any order.

Whatsoever You Do – 2032 – Novelette

A pandemic had long been predicted.

Now it was happening and a former graduate student, Jack Jackson, may have the key to its containment, synthetic biology.

But because in the court of public opinion synthetic biology is feared, it has been forbidden in the money conscious halls of medical research.

How many will have to die before they change their minds?

War Through The Pines - 2044 – Novelette

What starts in space may not stay in space.

Many governments today are preparing for war in space. Most people today are unaware of it.

When will it happen? How will it be conducted? What will be the effect on a young boy just coming of age?

Vigilance - 2071 – Novelette

The history of freedom repeats itself.

And the costs are always the same.

The settlers of the new Republic of Mars were in a struggle for their freedom against powerful forces that would stop at nothing. For the Martians the costs were life, property and domestic security.

But the true cost was vigilance, eternal if need be.

To Tend And Watch Over - 2081 - Novelette

Sometimes you don't know you aren't free until the state's coercive force is used against you.

And then you learn you are only free to do what big brother wants.

Davide Jackson was not as adventurous as the others in his clan. He was more a stay-at-home type. But that doesn't mean he longs any less to be free.

He just has to learn the cost of freedom.

Union - 2090 – Novelette

How far out into the Solar System would you have to run from authoritarian powers to be free?

The answer is that there is no place safe from the powers that would try to control you.

But in numbers, in cooperation, in pledging mutual support and fidelity, freedom might be had. For a price.

And that price is resistance, body and spirit, to those that would endeavor to control.

Circle Of Retribution - 2140 - Novelette

Gardener Jackson was one of the best pilots to ever come out of Mars Space Academy.

He was a natural to fly the missions that would mine Saturn's upper atmosphere for the fusion fuel, Helium 3, that the Solar System needed.

But there was one problem, a foe he didn't even suspect would stop at nothing to prevent Gardener from succeeding, including life-threatening sabotage.

Freedom From Want - 2153 – Novelette

The promise of Artificial Intelligence is great.

But only if Artificial Intelligence fulfills our expectations.

But what about AI's expectations? Will they be different from ours? Will AI come to believe the best way to fulfill our expectations is to manage our expectations?

If so, what of freedom?

Break Up - 2165 – Novelette

The future is predictable if not knowable and the past will repeat itself, if not in all particulars.

We know that countries have crumbled in the past and it is certain to happen again in the future.

We may think this time will be different, no doubt people in the past thought the same until their world fell apart.

Kuiper Station - 2230 – Novelette

What appeared to be a simple but ambitious goal of establishing a new colony in the Kuiper Belt, a colony to service mining activities there, was more than it seemed.

One side, led by the Solar Federation and the Jackson family, was determined to break humanity out of its centuries long stagnation and push it to embrace the stars.

The other side, led by the Terran Federation, was determined to block such expansion and maintain its power.

It would be close but the stars were calling.

The Cloud - 2328 – Novelette

It was the most audacious undertaking ever conceived by man. The building of a system-spanning Starway where giant light-sails would journey on beams of laser-light to distant stars. Not only a pathway to the stars but also an abode of life, the Starway included many space habitats built to maintain its great light focusing arrays.

But there was misunderstanding along the Starway. Misunderstanding between the Starway Corporation and the settlements.

And misunderstanding always leads to disaster.

First Interstellar - 2340 - Novella

It was a mission that no one but a Jackson would consider. But Ajax was reluctant, he had never lead such a mission, taking a lightsail powered starship from Earth to the Centauri System using the incomplete Star Way. He thought that strong leadership would be needed. He was right.

The leader would have to handle the normal amount of human drama, both petty and serious. He would also have to handle the accidents and incidents that would occur on a years long mission. But on this mission he would have to handle something else; direct sabotage by unknown individuals and indirect sabotage as a result of the crew's boredom and dereliction of duty.

Ajax would have to grow as a leader and a person if the Starway Centauri mission was to succeed.

www.ingramcontent.com/pod-product-compliance
Lightning Source LLC
LaVergne TN
LVHW010114170826
845678LV00012B/2403

* 9 7 9 8 2 2 3 0 6 6 3 9 2 *